# Cats Are Cats

## To Julie Amper and Grace Maccarone

Copyright © 2014 by Valeri Gorbachev
All Rights Reserved
HOLIDAY HOUSE is registered in the U.S. Patent and Trademark Office.
Printed and Bound in April 2014 at Tien Wah Press, Johor Bahru, Johor, Malaysia.
The artwork was created with watercolor and ink.
www.holidayhouse.com
First Edition
1 3 5 7 9 10 8 6 4 2

Library of Congress Cataloging-in-Publication Data
Gorbachev, Valeri, author, illustrator.
Cats are cats / Valeri Gorbachev. — First edition.
pages cm.
Summary: "Miss Bell loves her cat Tiger,
despite his tendency to act like a tiger"— Provided by publisher.
ISBN 978-0-8234-3052-9 (hardcover)
[1. Cats—Fiction. 2. Tigers—Fiction.
3. Pets—Fiction. 4. Humorous stories.] I. Title.
PZ7.G6475Car 2014
[E]—dc23
2013032896

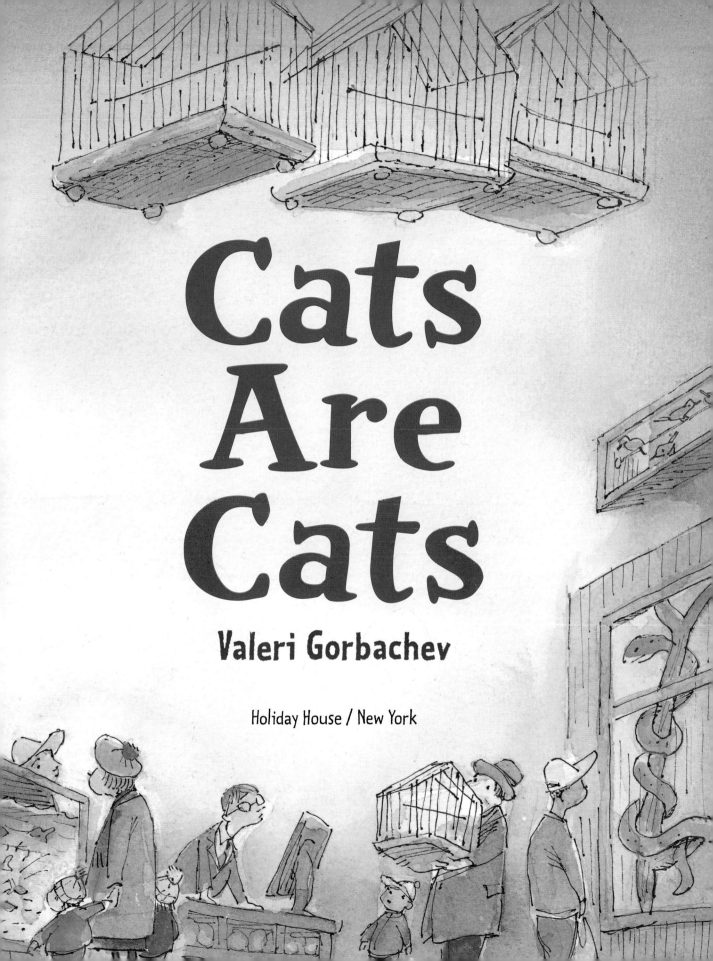

# Cats
# Are
# Cats

## Valeri Gorbachev

Holiday House / New York

Miss Bell loved cats.
One day she went to the
pet shop to get a little kitten.

He was very cute.
He had stripes like a tiger.
He had a tail like a tiger.

He had a smile like a tiger.
So Miss Bell named him Tiger.

She loved her little Tiger
very much.

She played with him.

She fed him.

She watched
TV with him.

Tiger grew
and grew
and grew.

He roared a big tiger roar.

Tiger took over
the whole house.

And sometimes
he made a big mess.

But he was still very cute,
and Miss Bell still loved
her Tiger.

"Cats are cats," she said.

One day they went for a walk.

Tiger stopped at the pet store.

"Cats are cats," Miss Bell said.
"They love fish!"

Tiger was happy.
He loved his fish.

One of his fish grew
and grew and grew.

But she was still very cute.
"Fish are fish," said Miss Bell.